# Measles and Sneezles

Compiled by

## Jennifer Curry

Illustrated by Susie Jenkin-Pearce

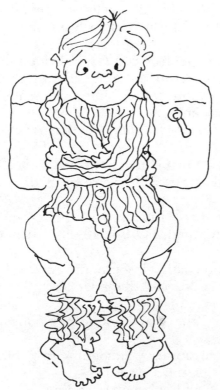

### Hutchinson
London   Sydney   Auckland   Johannesburg

*For my young friends and neighbours,*
*Thomas, Robert and Matthew*
*Kinsella*

Copyright © in this collection Jennifer Curry 1989
Copyright © Illustrations Susie Jenkin-Pearce 1989
*All rights reserved*
First published in Great Britain in 1989 by
Hutchinson Children's Books
An imprint of Century Hutchinson Ltd
Brookmount House, 62-65 Chandos Place,
Covent Garden, London WC2N 4NW

Century Hutchinson Australia (Pty) Ltd
20 Alfred Street, Milsons Point, Sydney 2061, Australia

Century Hutchinson New Zealand Limited
32-34 View Road, PO Box 40-086, Glenfield, Auckland 10

Century Hutchinson South Africa (Pty) Limited
PO Box 337, Bergvlei, 2012, South Africa

Printed and bound in Great Britain

British Library Cataloguing in Publication Data
Measles and sneezles.
    1. Children's poetry in English, 1945 – . Anthologies
    I. Curry, Jennifer II. Curry, Graeme
    821'.914'0809282

ISBN 0 09 174082 7

# First Word

## Sneezles

Christopher Robin
Had wheezles
And sneezles,
They bundled him
Into
His bed.
They gave him what goes
With a cold in the nose,
And some more for a cold
In the head.
They wondered
If wheezles
Could turn
Into measles,
If sneezles
Would turn
Into mumps;
They examined his chest
For a rash,
And the rest
Of his body for swellings and
lumps.

They sent for some doctors
In sneezles
And wheezles
To tell them what ought
To be done.

All sorts and conditions
Of famous physicians
Came hurrying round
At a run.
They all made a note
Of the state of his throat,
They asked if he suffered from thirst;
They asked if the sneezles
Came AFTER the wheezles,
Or if the first sneezle
Came first.
They said, 'If you teazle
A sneezle
Or wheezle,
A measle
May easily grow.
But humour or pleazle
The wheezle
Or sneezle,
The measle
Will certainly go.'
They expounded the reazles
For sneezles
And wheezles,
The manner of measles
When new.
They said, 'If he freezles

In draughts and in breezles,
Then PHTHEEZLES
May even ensue.'

Christopher Robin
Got up in the morning,
The sneezles had vanished away.
And the look in his eye
Seemed to say to the sky,
'Now, how to amuse them today?'

*A. A. Milne*

# Sneezes and Wheezes

# Oh no, I got a cold

I am sitting on the sofa,
By the fire and staying in,
Me head is free of comfort
And me nose is free of skin
Me friends have run for cover,
They have left me pale and sick
With me pockets full of tissues
And me nostrils full of Vick.

That bloke in the telly adverts,
He's supposed to have a cold,
He has a swig of whatnot
And he drops off, good as gold,
His face like snowing harvest
Slips into sweet repose,
Well, I bet this tortured breathing
Never whistled down his nose.

I burnt me bit of dinner
Cause I've lost me sense of smell
But then, I couldn't taste it
So that worked out very well.
I'd buy some, down the café
But I know that at the till
A voice from work will softly say
'I thought that you were ill.'

So I'm wrapped up in a blanket
With me feet up on a stool,
I've watched the telly programmes
And the kids come home from school,
But what I haven't watched for
Is any sympathy,
Cause all you ever get is:
'Oh no, keep away from me!'

Medicinal discovery,
It moves in mighty leaps,
It leapt straight past the common cold
And gave it us for keeps.
Now I'm not a fussy woman,
There's no malice in me eye
But I wish that they could cure
the common cold. That's all. Goodbye.

*Pam Ayres*

## Sniffle Skiffle

Mum and Dad
were once in a Skiffle Group
but Liz and I and Ted
have started a Sniffle Group.
We sneeze to each other in bed –
it's an old-fashioned Sniffle Skiffle
and what used to be called
A Cold In The Head!

*Gavin Ewart*

Skiffle was the Pop of the early Sixties, when
the Beatles first became famous, before the
days of synthesizers and electronic music.

## Ode to a sneeze

I sneezed a sneeze into the air.
It fell to earth I know not where,
But hard and froze were the looks of those
In whose vicinity I snooze.

*Anon.*

'Hello, hello, hello, sir,
   Meet me at the grocer.'
'No, sir.'
   'Why, sir?'
'Because I have a cold, sir.'
   'Where did you get your cold, sir?'
'At the North Pole, sir.'
   'What were you doing there, sir?'
'Catching polar bears, sir.'
   'Let me hear you sneeze, sir.'
'Tishoo, tishoo, tishoo, sir.'

*Traditional skipping game*

## My nose

It doesn't breathe;
It doesn't smell;
It doesn't feel
So very well.
I am discouraged
With my nose:
The only thing it
Does is blows.

*Dorothy Aldis*

Coughs and sneezes
Spread diseases.
*Slogan from the Second World War*

11

## Sneezing

Sneeze on Monday, sneeze for danger;
Sneeze on Tuesday, meet a stranger;
Sneeze on Wednesday, sneeze for a letter;
Sneeze on Thursday, something better;
Sneeze on Friday, sneeze for sorrow –
Sneeze on Saturday, see your sweetheart tomorrow.

*Traditional*

## Cough cough cough

Cough cough cough
Cough all day
Cough in the morning
Cough in the afternoon
Cough wherever I go
Even while I'm watching television
I – you know what – cough.

And I sneeze sometimes
But not very often.

*Oliver Gray (6)*

# Keep away from me

Please Jenny Penny, keep away from me,
I don't want to speak to you, nor you to speak to me.
Once we were friends, now we disagree,
Oh, Jenny Penny, keep away from me.
It's not because you're naughty,
It's nothing that you've said,
It's because you've got the whooping cough
And you should be in bed.

*Playground skipping game*

# Asthma attack

My little boy
Sits rigid on my lap
Fighting for breath.

His hair is damp with sweat.
His eyes are wide with fear.
His lungs whistle and wheeze
Like old and worn-out bellows.

Five years ago
My body gave life to his.
Now I long to pour my breath
Into his tiny frame
To give him peace and ease.

*Jenny Craig*

# Sniff

Caught a cold, sniff.
Feel all funny, sniff.
Eyes are red, sniff.
Nose is runny, sniff.
Can't complain, sniff.
I'm no fool, sniff.
One good thing, sniff.
Week off school . . .
   SNIFF.

*Colin McNaughton*

13

# A-shhoo!

Hay fever isn't at all funny.
You feel half-sick,
Your eyes are runny,
Your mouth is dry but your throat is thick.

Nice sunny day! But you start wheezing.
Your chest is sore
And now you're sneezing.
Atishhoo! Cough, and sneeze some more.

I'm dreaming, sitting here at school,
Of fresh blue sea
Or a swimming pool.
Such cool relief from this allergy.

But Teacher knows and she will say,
'You can stay in
When the others play,
And take your antihistamine.'

An all-grey sky, when it rains and rains,
Washing away
The pollen grains;
That's what *I* would call a perfect day.

*Robert Sparrow*

# Lots of Spots

# Spots!

The spots say it all –
chicken-pox!

My older sister says she's got spots –
but look at me!

She says having spots is very grown up –
does this mean I get a boyfriend?

I like it here, my father a doctor,
my mum a nurse – don't want to get better,
I want to get worse!

*Shaun Traynor*

## Measles

The few times back in the early fall
When kids had measles
And stayed home sick,
Our classroom teacher would have us all
Writing them letters
To get well quick.

But now, when most of the kids in school
Are out with measles
They somehow catch,
Our teacher's suddenly changed her rule
And just ignores them
And lets them scratch.

She says that lately we all get measle-y
MUCH too easily.

*Kaye Starbird*

17

## Chicken spots

I've got these really itchy spots
they're climbing on my tummy
they're on my head
they're on my tail
and it isn't very funny.
They came to see me yesterday
— a few the day before
fifty on my bottom
and twenty on my jaw.

I've got a prize one on my toe
a dozen on my knee
and now they're on my thingy
— I think there's thirty-three.

I count them every evening
I give them names like Fred
     Charlie Di and Daisy
     Chunky Tom and Ted.

They're really awful spotties
they drive me itchy mad
the sort of itchy scratchings
I wish I never had.
Nobby's worst at itching
Lizzie's awful too
and – if you come to see me
Then I'll give a few to you . . .
    I'll give you Di and Daisy –
    I'll give you Jane and Ted
    a bucket full of itchers
    to take home to your bed . . .
        You can give them to your sister
        I don't care what you do
        give them to a teacher
        or send them to the zoo.
        I don't care where you take 'em
        I don't care where they go . . .
            stick them up the chimney
            or in the baby's po.
            Take them to a farmyard.
            Find a chicken pen,
            say that they're a present

        with love
        from me

          . . to them.

*Peter Dixon*

# Feeling great!

I've been waiting for today.
Grandma's invited us to stay.
Mum wonders if we ought to go.
'Lots of illness round, you know.'

I shall climb Gran's apple trees,
Eat her home-grown strawberries.
Mum thinks I'm looking rather hot.
'It's all right, Mum. Of course I'm not.'

She'll make my favourite cherry cake,
Come fishing with me in the lake.
Mum asks if I'm really sure
I haven't got a temperature.

She'll feed me crusty home-baked bread,
Read me a story on my bed.
'Ought we to choose a later date?'
'Why Mum? What for? I'm feeling great.'

I thought that we were never going.
'Hullo Gran!' But she looks knowing.
'Come close, my lad. What are these lumps?'
'I can tell YOU! I've got the MUMPS!'

*Robert Sparrow*

## Sickness does come on horseback, but leave on foot

Yesterday I was jumping
Yesterday I was hopping
Yesterday I was body-popping
Yesterday I was doing bumps
on my bike,
just yesterday.

Now today
I got a real bad surprise
the doctor said I have mumps
I wake up with a sicky feeling
and water running from my eyes.
Granny said it must be fever,
the doctor said it's mumps.

Now I can't do bumps,
and Granny said, 'See what I mean,
just yesterday you been so up and about.
Now today the house so quiet.
Sickness does come on horseback,
but leave on foot.
Think about that while you lying in bed.'

I wish the stupid mumps
would jump on a bike
and don't bother come back.

*John Agard*

## Miss Dumps

Miss Dumps got the mumps
Didn't know where she got 'em,
Put her to bed with her feet at the head
And her nose sticking out at the
 bottom.

*Traditional playground rhyme*

## Two charms to cure warts

*Rub the wart gently against the bark of an ash tree and say:*

Ash tree, ashen tree,
Pray buy this wart of me.


Or, *while washing the hands in the moon's rays shining in a
dry metal basin, recite the following:*

I wash my hands in this thy dish,
Oh man in the moon, do grant my wish,
And come and take away this.

*Traditional*

## Mumps

I'm down in the dumps,
Because I've got mumps!
I hope it goes soon –
It's like a balloon!
It hurts when I yawn
And it hurts when I chew,
And sometimes I wish
That they'd change me for new!

Now DON'T call me fussy.
Because I am NOT!
I have to take tablets
And they make me hot!
I can't move around –
(That's unusual for me!)
I can't eat my breakfast,
My dinner . . . OR . . . tea!

I can't go to school
'cos my cheeks are so fat;
I look like a hamster –
I giggle at THAT!
I pull funny faces –
It helps pass the time;
I laid down and thought . . .
Then I made up this rhyme!

*Nicola Jane Field (9)*

## When I telephoned the school someone said . . .

Michelle's got the measles,
Matthew's got the mumps.
Richard says his throat's on fire,
And Jane's nose is out in lumps.

Simon has the jitters,
Susan has the shakes,
Wendy broke her forearm
Doing wheelies on her skates.

24

Nigel smashed his finger
Hammering nails in bits of wood,
Karen's got 'Artist's Tummy',
(Brian put paint in her food!)

Bouncing on the single bed
David broke six teeth,
His sister Kim is flat as a pancake –
She shouldn't have slept underneath!

Jeremy's nose is purple
His hands and feet are blue;
Shivering there in pyjamas –
Locked himself in the loo!

So there's no-one here but us teachers
So please phone back tonight,
The kids are all off with sickness

And   The HEAD   has just turned white.

*John Rice*


## There was a young lady

There was a young lady named Rose
Who had a huge wart on her nose;
When she had it removed
Her appearance improved,
But her glasses slipped down to her toes.

*Anon.*

## Spots

I've got spots.
I wish I hadn't, I'd rather I'd not,
I'll put up with a few but I've caught a whole lot:
Spots are what I've got.

I've got spots.
All over my body in thousands they lurk,
I've tried every ointment but none of them work:
Spots will drive me berserk.

I've got spots.
I have bathed in acanthus and extract of fern,
I've applied every lotion and potion in turn,
But still they itch and they burn.

I've got spots.
All I ask is a cream that will de-zit my skin,
But no sooner than I put the lid on the tin,
Once more those spots begin.

I *haven't* got spots.
Overnight by themselves they have vanished away,
I had hundreds last evening, but they've gone today,
So three cheers for my spots,
Shed no tears for my spots,
And let's hear for my spots:
'Hip hooray!'

*Christopher Mann*

# Rumbling Bowels

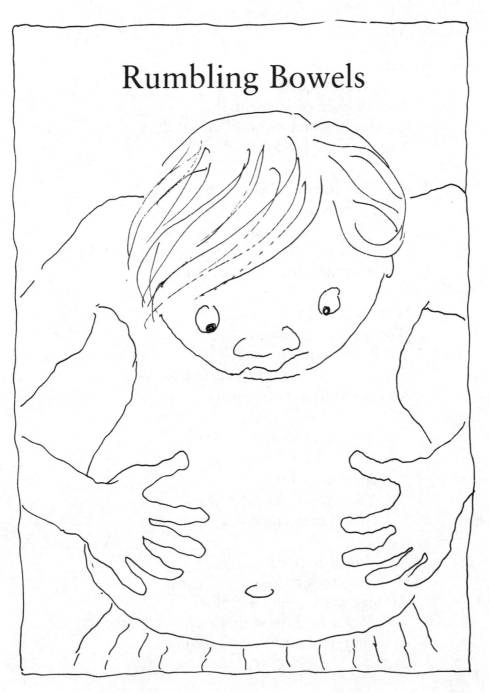

# Maveric

Maveric Prowles
Had Rumbling Bowles
That thundered in the night.
It shook the bedrooms all around
And gave the folks a fright.

The doctor called;
He was appalled
When through his stethoscope
He heard the sound of a baying hound,
And the acrid smell of smoke.

Was there a cure?
'The higher the fewer,'
The learned doctor said,
Then turned poor Maveric inside out
And stood him on his head.

'Just as I thought
You've been and caught
An Asiatic flu —
You mustn't go near dogs I fear
Unless they come near you.'

Poor Maveric cried.
He went cross-eyed,
His legs went green and blue.
The doctor hit him with a club
And charged him one and two.

And so my friend
This is the end,
A warning to the few:
Stay clear of doctors to the end
Or they'll get rid of you.

*Spike Milligan*

## Job satisfaction

I am a young bacterium
And I enjoy my work
I snuggle into people's food
I lie in wait – I lurk.
They chomp a bit and chew a bit
And say, 'This can't be beaten'
But then in bed they groan and moan;
'I wish I hadn't eaten.'

*John Collins*

## A stomach-ache is worse away from home

'Sir,' I said,
Hoping for sympathy,
'I've got the stomach-ache.'
All of it was true,
There was no putting it on.
I gave out winces with my mouth
Using my eyebrows skilfully
And held the hurt place hard
With both hands.
But it was my white face convinced him.
So he sent me outside
To walk it away in the fresh air.
Outside it was deathly cold.
Because he had his hand up first
Trev came out too
To see I was all right.
A grey wind with rain in it
Whipped across the playground,
Spattering through puddles.
And setting the empties rolling
Up and down, up and down
And clatter-rattling in their crates.
Trev said, 'You'll be alright.'
And started kicking a tennis ball
Up against the toilet wall,
His hands in his pockets,
Bent against the cold.

The dinner ladies came out.
Moaning slightly I bent over
And gritted my teeth bravely.
But they didn't see
And walked through the school gates laughing.
At home there would be the smell of cooking
And our Robbo asleep before the fire.
I looked through the railings
And thought my way to our house.
Past the crumbling wall,
The Bingo Hall,
The scraggy tree
As thin as me,
The rotting boarding
By the cinema
With last week's star
In a Yankee car
Flapping on the hoarding.
Stop!
Turn right towards town
And three doors down,
That's our house.

*Gareth Owen*

# Mary had a little lamb

Mary had a little lamb,
    A lobster and some prunes,
A glass of milk, a piece of pie,
    And then some macaroons.

It made the busy waiters grin
    To see her order so,
And when they carried Mary out,
    Her face was white as snow.

*Anon.*

Mary ate jam,
Mary ate jelly,
Mary went home
With a pain in her —
Now don't get excited
Don't be misled
Mary went home
With a pain in her head.

*Playground rhyme*

Mother made a seedy cake,
Gave us all the belly ache;
Father bought a pint of beer,
Gave us all the diarrhoea.

*Playground rhyme*

34

## Two charms to cure hiccups

Hiccup, hiccup, go away,
Come again another day:
Hiccup, hiccup, when I bake,
I'll make you a butter-cake.

Hiccup, snickup,
Rise up, right up,
Three drops in a cup
Goodbye, hiccup.

*Traditional*

35

# Henry King

*Who Chewed Bits of String,*
*and was early Cut Off in Dreadful Agonies*

The Chief Defect of Henry King
Was chewing little bits of String.
At last he swallowed some which tied
Itself in ugly Knots inside.
Physicians of the Utmost Fame
Were called at once; but when they came
They answered, as they took their Fees:
'There is no Cure for this Disease.

Henry will very soon be dead.'
His Parents stood about his Bed
Lamenting his Untimely Death,
When Henry, with his Latest Breath,
Cried: 'Oh, my Friends, be warned by me,
That Breakfast, Dinner, Lunch, and Tea
Are all the Human Frame requires . . .'
With that the Wretched Child expires.

*Hilaire Belloc*

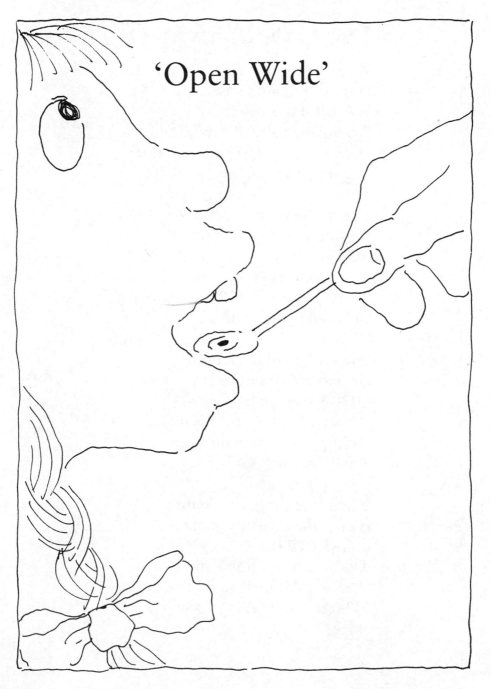

'Open Wide'

# Visit to the dentist

When Ulie woke up
He had the toothache.
  AARGH!
'Too many sweets!' said his mam.
'Never cleans 'em!' said his gran.
'Listen who's talking!' said U.

When Ulie went to school
He still had the toothache.
  EEEGH!
'Ulie's making noises!' said Jason.
'Ulie's pulling faces!' said Alice.
'So would *you*!' said U.

When Ulie got back home
He was trying not to cry.
  O-O-OH!
'To the dentist!' said his mam.
'Told you so!' said his gran.
'Oh, leave off!' said U.

When Ulie sat in the chair
He felt the dentist's probe.
  GARRGH!
'Do sit still!' said the nurse.
'This won't hurt!' said the dentist.
'Who're you kidding?' said U.

When Ulie saw the drill
He bit the dentist's hand.
   SCREECH!
'You need a smack!' said the nurse.
'Your teeth will rot!' said the dentist.
'I don't care!' said U.

When Ulie felt the needle
He suddenly went numb.
   AH-HUM!
'Open wide!' said the dentist.
'All over now!' said the nurse.
'Nothing to it!' said U.

*Jennifer Curry*

## Clinical clerihew (1)

MR WILLIAM CLARK

Mr William Clark
(a certain Yankee dentist) made his mark
By knocking out his patients with some ether
And thus became the first no-fuss de-teether.

*Christopher Mann*

A *clerihew* is a four-line poem, called after the man who invented it, Edmund
Clerihew Bentley. Lines one and two rhyme with each other, and so do lines
three and four, and together they tell you something important about the person
whose name is in the first line.

# Thoughts from a dentist's waiting room

Please let there be a powercut.
Just a tiny little one.
Just before he gets the drill near my mouth.

One down, two to go

Or maybe he'll be struck down,
By a hitherto undiscovered and as yet incurable
palsy
which only lasts for the ten minutes I'm with him,
and then vanishes forever?

Two down, one to go

Maybe he got the notes mixed up.
'Ridiculous,' he'll say, 'You don't need fillings at all!'
'They're old Mrs Crabtree's notes!' (even though
she has dentures).

NEXT PLEASE!

Why is the dentist the only one who is ever smiling?

*Amanda Evans (14)*

A dentist named Archibald Moss
Fell in love with the dainty Miss Ross.
Since he held in abhorrence
Her Christian name, Florence,
He renamed her his dear dental Floss

*Anon.*

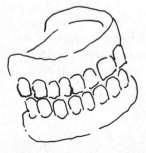

# A thought

When we are hungry we eat sweets and
When the sweets are hungry they eat our teeth.

*Mark Raven (8)*

# A charm against the toothache

Venerable Mother Toothache
Climb down from the white battlements,
Stop twisting in your yellow fingers
The fourfold rope of nerves;
And tomorrow I will give you a tot of whisky
To hold in your cupped hands,
A garland of anise-flowers,
And three cloves like nails.

And tell the attendant gnomes
It is time to knock off now,
To shoulder their little pick-axes,
Their cold-chisels and drills,
And you may mount by a silver ladder
Into the sky, to grind
In the cracked polished mortar
Of the hollow moon.

By the lapse of warm waters,
And the poppies nodding like red coals,
The paths on the granite mountains,
And the plantation of my dreams.

*John Heath-Stubbs*

## Oh, I wish
## I'd looked after me teeth

Oh, I wish I'd looked after me teeth,
   And spotted the perils beneath,
All the toffees I chewed,
   And the sweet sticky food,
Oh, I wish I'd looked after me teeth.

I wish I'd been that much more willin'
   When I had more tooth there than fillin'
To pass up gobstoppers,
   From respect to me choppers
And to buy something else with me
   shillin'.

When I think of the lollies I licked,
   And the liquorice allsorts I picked,
Sherbet dabs, big and little,
   All that hard peanut brittle,
My conscience gets horribly pricked.

My Mother, she told me no end,
   'If you got a tooth, you got a friend.'
I was young then, and careless,
   My toothbrush was hairless,
I never had much time to spend.

Oh I showed them the toothpaste all right,
   I flashed it about late at night,
But up-and-down brushin'
   And pokin' and fussin'
Didn't seem worth the time – I could bite!

If I'd known I was paving the way,
   To cavities, caps and decay,
The murder of fillin's
   Injections and drillin's
I'd have thrown all me sherbet away.

So I lay in the old dentist's chair,
   And I gaze up his nose in despair,
And his drill it do whine,
   In these molars of mine,
'Two amalgam,' he'll say, 'for in there.'

How I laughed at my Mother's false teeth,
   As they foamed in the waters beneath,
But now comes the reckonin'
   It's *me* they are beckonin'
Oh, I *wish* I'd looked after me teeth.

                              *Pam Ayres*

## Having a brace

I sit on the chair, my legs shaking
He takes it out of the impression.
I look at it. It's pink and silver.
I feel butterflies in my stomach.

He puts it in my mouth
I can't swallow
Half choking me he takes it out
He looks at it.

I am thinking,
what will people say?
How will I eat?
Will it be strange?
Will I be able to speak?

He puts it back in my mouth
I am beginning to be able to swallow
I learned to take it in and out
Then he says we can go.

Feeling as if I have a sweet in my mouth
I put on a brave face
And go out to meet my problems.

*Karen Elkington (9)*

# Don't Fall Out of Windows

## Advice to small children

Eat no green apples or you'll droop,
Be careful not to get the croup,
Avoid the chicken-pox and such,
And don't fall out of windows
    much.

*Edward Anthony*

## Wendy in winter

No wonder Wendy's coat blew off.
She didn't have it zipped.
And – since she didn't watch for slush –
No wonder Wendy slipped.
No wonder Wendy froze her feet
Although her boots were lined,
Because when Wendy left for school
She left her boots behind.
And since she didn't dodge the ice
That sagged an apple bough,
No wonder Wendy's hatless head
Has seven stitches now.

*Kaye Starbird*

## My head

Near my head lies the world;
My head is like an egg but delicate,
It can be broken easily.

*Erika Cottle (7)*

46

## All aboard

I carry my friends like a crew on a ship.
They say they're all there; that no-one's been missed.
They have all signed their names in coloured felt-tip,
Over my plaster, from elbow to wrist.

There's Denis and Geoffrey and Arthur and Wayne,
Andrew and Henry, and new Carolyn;
And Josephine, Alice and Mary and Jane,
Peter, and Paul, his identical twin.

And Freda and Laurence and Tony and Nell,
Robert and Rachel, and Alan and Tim;
'Brains' Alexander, and his sister Michelle.
(She can play football much better than him.)

My sister has printed I, L, E, E, N.
She's only five so her spelling's not good.
Here's Willoughby, (Honest!) Edward and Ben,
And once again:– Wayne; Of course, but *he* would.

I've just found a name that I don't really know.
A girl? Or a boy? Find out if I can.
Who was the person who wrote 'J' and 'O'?
'Your best mate. Who else? It's me, Jonathan.

The others all wrote and left only one space.
Now you're my best friend. Don't mean any harm.
But bags I to write in the very first place,
The next time you think of breaking your arm.'

*Robert Sparrow*

## An accident

The playground noise stilled.
A teacher ran to the spot
beneath the climbing frame
where Rawinda lay, motionless.
We crowded around, silent,
gazing at the trickle of bood
oozing its way on to the tarmac.
Red-faced, the teacher shouted,
'Move back . . . get out of the way!'
and carried Rawinda into school,
limbs floppy as a rag doll's,
a red gash on her black face.

Later we heard she was at home,
five stitches in her forehead.
After school that day
Jane and I stopped beside the frame
and stared at the dark stain
shaped like a map of Ireland.
'Doesn't look much like blood,'
muttered Jane. I shrugged,
and remember now how warm it was
that afternoon, the white clouds,
and how sunlight glinted
from the polished bars.

We took Rawinda's 'Get Well' card
to her house. She was in bed,
quiet, propped up on pillows,

a white plaster on her dark skin.
Three days later
she was back at school,
her usual self, laughing,
twirling expertly on the bars,
wearing her plaster with pride,
covering for a week the scar
she would keep for ever,
memento of a July day at school.

*Wes Magee*


## Oh to be

Oh to be a broken leg
In plaster white as chalk
And travel everywhere by crutch
While others have to walk.

*Mike Griffin*


## Mind and matter

There was a faith-healer of Deal,
Who said, 'Although pain isn't real,
   If I sit on a pin
   And it punctures my skin,
I dislike what I fancy I feel.'

*Anon.*

## Dad's pigeon

Now pigeon-racing is a sport
That dad was keen on trying.
Alas, the bird that daddy bought
Was terrified of flying.

'Well, who's a pretty pigeon then?'
Said daddy, as he threw it.
The pigeon fell to earth again;
'You twit!' cried dad. 'You blew it!'

'You've got to flap your wings,' said dad.
'Now practise, get acquainted!'
The pigeon flapped its wings like mad,
Took off, then promptly fainted.

To help the pigeon understand
Dad gave a demonstration,
He flapped, he jumped and came to land
In mother's rose plantation.

My dad is slowly on the mend,
My mother's still in shock,
And me? I take our feathered friend
For walkies round the block.

                    *Doug MacLeod*

# Three ruthless rhymes

Bob was bathing in the Bay,
When a Shark who passed that way
Punctured him in seven places;
– And he made SUCH funny faces!

Auntie, did you feel no pain
    Falling from the apple tree?
Will you do it, please, again?
    'Cos my friend here didn't see.

A window cleaner in our street
Who fell (five storeys) at my feet
Impaled himself on my umbrella.
I said, 'Come, come, you careless fella!
If my umbrella had been shut
You might have landed on my nut!'

*Harry Graham*

# A boy of Baghdad

There once was a boy of Baghdad
An inquisitive sort of a lad.
    He said, 'I will see
    If a sting has a bee.'
And he very soon found that it had.

*Anon.*

51

## Well ill

I felt OK this morning
When I got out of bed.
Now I've got this blinkin paper bag
Stuck on me blinkin head.

I keep on smelling fish and chips
Or cider going bad.
Or it might be pickled onions –
I shall have to ask me dad.

I wish I could remember
How I came to feel so ill.
Have I had some sort of accident?
Where is Dad – and Mum – and Jill?

I would love a drink of water
But there's nothing in the pail
I shall have to climb that blinkin hill
And use the blinkin well!

But I'll never manage by meself
I feel so blinkin ill.
Who's going to help me with the pail?
Where's Mum? Where's Dad? Where's Jill?

Right! I'm goin' down the Water Board.
We're having runnin water!
I'll say me Dad'll pay for it –
They won't tumble till after!

I shall leave a little note out.
When the three of them get back
They'll get the blinkin message
Sayin, *'I'm all right now. Jack.'*

Ian Whybrow

## Nettles

My son aged three fell in the nettle bed.
'Bed' seemed a curious name for those green spears,
That regiment of spite behind the shed:
It was no place for rest. With sobs and tears
The boy came seeking comfort and I saw
White blisters beaded on his tender skin.
We soothed him till his pain was not so raw.
At last he offered us a watery grin,
And then I took my hook and honed the blade
And went outside and slashed in fury with it
Till not a nettle in that fierce parade
Stood upright any more. Next task: I lit
A funeral pyre to burn the fallen dead.
But in two weeks the busy sun and rain
Had called up tall recruits behind the shed:
My son would often feel sharp wounds again.

Vernon Scannell

## Tracey's tree

Last year it was not there,
the sapling with purplish leaves
planted in our school grounds with care.
It's Tracey's tree, my friend who died,
and last year it was not there.

Tracey, the girl with long black hair
who, out playing one day, ran
across a main road for a dare.
The lorry struck her. Now a tree grows
and last year it was not there.

Through the classroom window I stare
and watch the sapling sway.
Soon its branches will stand bare.
It wears a forlorn and lonely look
and last year it was not there.

October's chill is in the air
and cold rain distorts my view.
I feel a sadness that's hard to bear.
The tree blurs, as if I've been crying,
and last year it was not there.

Wes Magee

# Tucked Up in Bed

# The land of counterpane

When I was sick and lay a-bed,
I had two pillows at my head,
And all my toys beside me lay
To keep me happy all the day.

And sometimes for an hour or so
I watched my leaden soldiers go,
With different uniforms and drills,
Among the bedclothes, through the hills;

And sometimes sent my ships in fleets
All up and down among the sheets;
Or brought my trees and houses out,
And planted cities all about.

I was the giant great and still
That sits upon the pillow-hill,
And sees before him, dale and plain,
The pleasant land of counterpane.

*Robert Louis Stevenson*

# Limerick in bed

When I was kept lying in bed
With an ache in my heart and my head
  My knees made high hills
  To hide biscuits and pills
Under books which I still haven't read.

*Jane Whittle*

56

## Be careful

Be careful when you cross the road,
Be careful when you swim,
Be careful when you climb a tree,
Be careful when you crim.

I crimmed last week and look at me,
All coddled up in bed
With awful toothache in my ears
And heartburn in my head.

My nose is stiff, my tummy sings,
My legs have got the flu,
I can't read books without my eyes,
My neck keeps going; 'Atchoo!'

The doctor give me orange pills
To take when I'm asleep,
My knees won't touch my shoulder blades
And now my back's too steep.

My right hand's where my left should be
My thumbs don't make a sound,
There's something pink inside my mouth,
My breath's the wrong way round.

So learn from me and my mistake:
Be careful when you swim
Or climb a tree, but most of all,
Be careful when you crim.

*Richard Edwards*

# The Kangaroo's Coff

*A Poem for Children Ill in Bed, Indicating to Them the Oddities of our English Orthography*

The eminent Professor Hoff
Kept, as a pet, a Kangaroo
Who, one March day, started a coff
That very soon turned into floo.

Before the flu carried him off
To hospital (still with his coff),
A messenger came panting through
The door, and saw the Kangarough.

The Kangaroo lay wanly there
Within the Prof's best big armchere,
Taking (without the power to chew)
A sip of lemonade or tew.

'O Kangaroo,' the fellow said,
'I'm glad you're not already daid,
For I have here (pray do not scoff)
Some stuff for your infernal coff.

'If you will take these powdered fleas,
And just a tiny lemon squeas
Mixed with a little plain tapwater,
They'll cure you. Or at least they ater.'

Prof Hoff then fixed the medicine,
Putting the fleas and lemon ine
A glass of water, which he brought
The Kangaroo as he'd been tought.

The Kangaroo drank down the draught,
Shivered and scowled — then oddly laught
And vaulted out of the armchair
Before the Prof's astonished stair —

Out of the window, in the air,
Up to the highest treetop whair
He sat upon the topmost bough
And chortled down, 'Look at me nough!'

The messenger would not receive
Reward for this, but answered, 'Weive
Done our best, and that's reward
Enough, my very learned lard'

(By which he meant Professor Hoff).
As for the Kangaroo, he blew
A kiss down as the man rode off,
A cured and happy Kangarew —

As you may be, when you have read
This tale I wrote lying in bed.

*Anthony Thwaite*

*Note: orthography* means spelling

59

## What's wrong with me?

The strait-jacket of the sheets
so grannily tucked in,
The day's minutes heart-beating
like a hospital drip on my digital clock,
the shrieks of children at playtime
in playgrounds near to me, regular as medicine,
make me sick!

Thank God for clouds!
Through the kaleidoscope-shaped window,
mercifully cut into the wall of my illness,
I watch them, give them names:
old man with beard 1, old man with beard 2,
old man with beard and banana-skin-feet 3 . . .
the wispy ones are like words in a two-day-sentence,
sometimes put in the wrong order, always in code,
sometimes they mean, 'Can you come out to play?'
Or sometimes I think, perhaps, they are talking
to someone else. I would like to form a society,
Friends of the Cloud-keeper, *only sick people need
    apply . . .*

The doctor, grey and over-worked, face-lined,
comes at four o'clock. I'm the last
of his morning calls! He murmurs to my mum
after his sweaty hands have felt all over me –
'She'll survive,' through his Fisherman's-Friends,
bad, adult breath. They both laugh
out of a mutually hypocritical politeness
and I smile like I had curls on my forehead.

He, going out, meets my brothers and sisters coming in;
they visit me in dribs and drabs with tales
of another lunch-time detention for Gail
and other forms of teacher-torture.
I miss my teacher. Don't miss Gail.
My brothers and sisters have hamburger buns and tea for
   supper
if my nose does not deceive me –
I get spoon-fed fish and hot milk,
is this what it's like to be old?
I mean, older than granny?
Spoon-fed, helped to the toilet,
wiped, tucked in again, help!
I'm not ready yet
to give up the ghost!

The TV my parents specially rented for me
is really hotting up now!
When I'm better I'll appear on ARMCHAIR CRITICS'
   QUESTION TIME
and win £1,000 – pathetic!
Sleep comes like an amalgam
of Terry Wogan, L.A. Law, Points of View,
it arrives
on a tablet and in a tiny sachet of power –

the last thing I remember
is a loving kiss goodnight –

What's wrong with me?

*Shaun Traynor*

61

## Invalid

Such a commotion
Coming up off the street,
Such a shouting and calling
Such a running of feet.
Such a rolling of marbles
Such a whipping of tops
Such a skipping of skips
Such a hopping of hops –
And I'm in bed.

So much chasing and fighting
Down on the street
Such a claiming of victories
Such howling defeats.
So much punching and shoving
So much threatening to clout
So much running to doorways
Until it's safe to come out –
But I'm in bed.

So much hiding and seeking
From the pavement below
So much argy bargy
Who'll hide and whose go.
Such a throwing of balls
Such picking of sides
Such a racing of bikes
Such a begging of rides –
And I'm in bed.

If I was a dictator
And the world was a street
There'd be no more homework
No school dinners to eat.
I'd abolish exams
I'd banish all sums
And we'd play in a street
Where night never comes –
And I'd never be ill.

*Gareth Owen*

## Clinical clerihew (2)

MR ALEXANDER GRAHAM BELL

Mr Alexander Graham Bell
(though not a doctor), when he wasn't well
Found it irksome to be kept alone
So he invented the telephone.

*Christopher Mann*

## Big day

Playing for the School today;
Ten minutes to the start of play;
Run out on the football ground,
Kick the practice ball around.

Time now for the Captains' call;
We take the kick, I've got the ball.
Fool that winger. Spring on ahead,
Draw two defence and pass to Ted.

He foot-traps. Holds. I've marked a space;
Ted flicks to Nick; I start to race;
Nick slides a low one to my feet.
Here comes the back. Just him to beat.

Watch the goalie, let the ball roll;
He runs forward. Shoot! It's a goal!
No it isn't. I'm sick in bed.
'Up tomorrow,' the Doctor said.

To make things worse. Great spots of rain
Spatter over the window pane.
Rain! That's no little April shower.
Been roaring down now, half an hour.

I hear the phone ring in the hall
And Mum's voice saying, 'I'll tell Paul.'
'A flooded pitch. Fit for a duck.'
(Poor chaps, that really is bad luck.)

A flooded pitch! No chance of play!
The Match put off a week today!
I should be fit then for the Team.
Perhaps I'll score, as in my dream!

*Robert Sparrow*

## It's cold in my room

It's cold in my room,
and the shadows jump on the walls,
and the window rattles,
and the curtain moves its limbs
in a dance.

It's quiet in my room,
and the blanket folds me to the bed,
and the window swings,
and the mirror turns to see my face
in a glance.

It's warm in my room,
and the sunlight blares like a trumpet,
and the window glows,
and the leaves flutter from the branches
in advance.

It's dark in my room,
and the stars glitter in the darkness,
and the window beckons,
and the night breeze sings its little song
in the silence.

*Christopher Mann*

## When Dad felt bad

One Sunday, Dad was feeling bad.
Pains in his head and tum, Mum said.

No dinner, Mum.
My head! My tum!

Dad said,
I bet
it's what I ate.

Too much to drink
said Mum,
I think.
Poor old chap,
Let him take a nap.

Then our cat, Ted,
jumped on the bed,
and put a mole
on poor Dad's head.

Dad jumped right up,
pyjamas down.
They heard him yell
all over town.

Quick! Quick!
said Dad.
Bring a big tin.

We put it down.
The mole ran in.

Down by the tree,
Dad set it free.

That's good, said Dad.
Now I feel fine.
I wonder if
it's dinner-time?

*Charles Causley*

# Doctor! Doctor!

## Miss Polly

Miss Polly had a dolly
who was sick, sick, sick.
So she sent for the doctor
to come quick, quick, quick.
The doctor came
with his bag and his hat
and he knocked at the door
with a rat-a-tat-tat.
He looked at the dolly
and he shook his head
and he said, 'Miss Polly,
put her straight to bed.'
He wrote down on a paper
for a pill, pill, pill.
'I'll be back in the morning
with the bill, bill, bill.'

*Anon.*

## Four doctors

Four doctors tackled Johnny Smith –
  They blistered and they bled him;
With squills and antibilious pills
  And ipecac. they fed him.
They stirred him up with calomel,
  And tried to move his liver;
But all in vain – his little soul
  Was wafted o'er The River.

*Max Adeler*

68

## Fresh air

In 1902
Miss Molly got flu,

So the doctor came
With his bag and his cane.

He took off his coat
And peered down her throat.

He lifted her vest
And tapped on her chest.

He felt her hot brow
And murmured, 'Now! now!

I know your throat's sore
But I've told you before,

It's fresh AIR that you need,
Or those nasty germs breed.

This window's tight shut!'
He uttered, 'Tut! TUT!'

Then he lifted his stick
And gave a quick flick.

With one blow of his cane
He shattered the pane.

Glass flew far and wide.
Fresh air rushed inside.

'That's better!' he said,
'Better draughty than dead!'

*Tym Hattersley*

69

# Hardly himself

'That's not like Jack,' his Father said.
'He's much too quiet, I am sure;
Not wrestling with his brother Fred,
And didn't even slam the door.
Not like Jack at all.' he said.

'That's not like Jack,' his Mother said.
'To sit there staring at his tea,
And say he'd like to go to bed;
Not stay up late and watch TV.
Not like Jack at all.' she said.

'That's not like Jack,' his Sister said.
'Not bothering to tweak my hair.
Just sits and tugs his own instead,
Huddling in the easy chair.
Not like Jack at all.' she said.

'A poor old Jack,' the Doctor said.
'He does look miserable and grey!
Now wrap up warm and stay in bed.
Pink medicine, three times a day.
Not your Jack at all.' he said.

'Is that our Jack?' his Mother said.
'Does he want help? What are those thumps?
And all that banging overhead?
I keep on hearing thuds and bumps.
See if Jack's all right.' she said.

'That *is* like Jack,' the Family said.
He's doing forward rolls and flips,
And bouncing up and down his bed;
Yelling *I want sausages and chips.*
That's the Jack *we* know.' they said.

*Robert Sparrow*

## A visit to the doctor

I went to the doctor's
And guess what I had!

I had spots on my bots,
And splinters in my knickers,
And I hid in the loo
Because I had flu,
And tonsillitis
And fleabiters.
I was down in the dumps
Because I had mumps
And bumps
And lumps,
And even my toy beaver
Had a dose of the fever.

The doctor said, 'Try these!
Here's pink pills and green pills and blue pills
And horrible medicine.'
Ugh!

*Robin Gillyon (7)*

# I have a little cough, sir

'I have a little cough, sir,
   In my little chest, sir,
All night long I cough, sir,
   I can never rest, sir.

And every time I cough, sir,
   It leaves a little pain, sir.
Cough! Cough! Cough! sir,
   There it goes again, sir.

Oh, doctor, doctor,
   I shall surely die!'

'Yes, my pretty little dear –
And so, one day, shall I!'

*Traditional playground rhyme*


# Doctor Bell

Doctor Bell fell down the well
And broke his collar-bone.
Doctors should attend the
   sick
And leave the well alone.

*Anon.*

# You can take my blood

Doctor you can take my blood out
Doctor doctor I said
Take my blood out.
You can have some
If you want it.
To put in someone else.

*Edward Cooper (7)*

# Calling the doctor

Doctor! Doctor!
I've got trouble with my nose!
Doctor! Doctor!
I've got trouble with my toes
Doctor! Doctor!
I've got trouble with my head!
Doctor! Doctor!
I'm stopping in bed.

*John Cunliffe*

# Clinical clerihew (3)

SIR ALEXANDER FLEMING

Fleming, Sir Alexander
(No relation to Ian, the naval commander
and author of spy books exotic);
Discovered penicillin, the number one antibiotic.

*Christopher Mann*

# Ear-ache

*(for Tym.)*

One of my tenderest memories from childhood
is having ear-ache; the pain was terrible
but the sympathy from Gran and mum
and head-turning dad
was immeasurable!

Gran and mum got warm butter and olive oil,
an eye-bowl, mixed it all together with cotton-wool
and placed the comforting poultice inside my ear-hole;

the warmth permeated my brain,
was like the hot-water bottle that warmed my tummy,
I slept in a cocoon of love:

they told me the doctor had come,
had felt my forehead, they paid him
with six warm eggs.

In the morning the world was cold,
the pollen-embedded ice-berg of cotton-wool
was hard and solidified, it drew out all the badness,
my forehead was chill.

I got dressed, no pain, good equilibrium,
dad said, 'this child is fit for school!'

Shaun Traynor

74

Mother, mother, I am ill,
Send for the doctor from over the hill.
In comes the doctor,
In comes the nurse,
In comes the lady with the alligator purse.
Penicillin, says the doctor,
Penicillin, says the nurse,
Penicillin, says the lady with the alligator purse.

*Traditional skipping game*

## Headache

That one I had yesterday was a *blinder*.
Pointless going to school.
Hardly left me strength to turn on the radio.
It came from somewhere deep,
(I can't tell you precisely where:
You know how it is with these things.)
It made me feel as if I was going
Downstairs too fast
In a pair of heavy shoes
And my brain started jerking
Like a jellyfish, swirling,
Like a shirt in the wash.
Every time it swung round, the front
Button and zips bashed the back of my eyes.
I'm not sure I didn't have swollen glands.
No, I didn't see the doctor.
Anyway, Saturday today.
Yes. A lot better, thanks.

*Ian Whybrow*

## An injection

We stampede down the corridor,
Each holding a white card,
Fingering it like some poisonous insect.
Will it hurt?
The thud of our feet echoes our drumming hearts.
'Bags last!'
'I'm going last.'
'I'm not going first.'
'Me neither.'
We stand in line,
Like prisoners waiting for execution.
I'm not scared.
I try to sound heroic.
I drift . . .
Into a senseless dream.
I snap out of it as my friend jolts me.
Saying, 'Go on, it's you next.'
I march stiffly towards the door.
The nurse motions me to the chair.
The saliva refuses to enter my mouth.
The blue-flamed bunsen-burner hisses slightly.
The drab, grey walls seem more depressing than usual.
My sleeve is pushed roughly up.
The strong stench of disinfectant bites my nostrils.
My arm is touched with something cold.
I shudder violently.
It brushes my arm
Soothingly.
Everyone falls silent.
It's over!

A mere pin prick.
A bubble of blood
Dribbles down my arm.
It's absorbed by a piece of lint.
A gush of breath rushes out.
The air seems clearer.
My mind fresher.
  'Next please.'

*Janet Clark (12)*

## Tom's song

With arching back
And reddened cheeks
The baby twists
And turns and shrieks
As mother counters
Coaxing, pleading,
'Medicine's nice'
She thinks she's winning.
Thomas smiles and shuts his mouth –
Then spits the bright pink liquid out.

*Barry Norrington*


## Taking medicine

In the bedroom I hide,
Mother calls,
My sister reads,
And I am silent,
I go to her very gravely going as silently and slowly as I can,
Suddenly I rush into the kitchen,

I say, quick, to get it over and done with,
With hot eyes I see mother pouring it out,
I bite the spoon the last drop,
Here I go,
When I have finished I run up the hall shouting,
'I have had my medicine go and have yours.'

*Valerie Seekings*

# In Hospital

# Children imagining a hospital

*For Kingswood County Primary School*

I would like kindness, assurance,
A wide selection of books;
Lots of visitors, and a friend
To come and see me:
A bed by the window so I could look at
All the trees and fields, where I could go for a walk.
I'd like a hospital with popcorn to eat.
A place where I have my own way.

I would like HTV all to myself.
And people bringing tea round on trollies;
Plenty of presents and plenty of cards
(I would like presents of food).
Things on the walls, like pictures, and things
That hang from the ceiling;
Long corridors to whizz down in wheelchairs.
Not to be left alone.

U. A. Fanthorpe

80

## Hospital

The white walls, echoing, lonely corridors
Seem unwelcoming for a caring place.
The staring nurses and patients,
The abrupt and brief talk with the lean
Lady behind reception, her glasses distorting the reflections
    of the gathering place.
A quick rush for the playing area, but
your mother's firm hand pressing on your shoulder
    automatically suggesting no.
The sitting down on a hard red chair, still
Warm, with the shape of the previous person still
    embedded.
The harsh, 'Next one please,' that turns out
to be all right, for doctor with the
Most warming smile says:
'And what's wrong with you then?'

*Brian Geary (15)*

# And how are we today?

'Hello, and how are we today?'
I feel as if I'm going to die.
'I'm fine.' There's nothing else to say.

Who would listen anyway
if I found the right reply?
'Hello, and how are we today?'

Came round again on Saturday
and all I managed was a sigh,
'I'm fine.' There's nothing else to say.

I can't get up, go out to play.
Next time he comes I'll ask him why.
'Hello, and how are we today?'

Next time I may have run away.
In here I never see the sky.
'I'm fine.' There's nothing else to say.

I wasn't home by Christmas Day.
'Goodbye, good luck!' 'Take care, goodbye!'
'Hello, and how are we today?'
'I'm fine.' There's nothing else to say.

*Jane Whittle*

# Dr. Christmas

My first thought: 'Have they sterilised the beard
Worn by so many Father Christmases
Before me?' Then: 'These children, they've just heard
My voice, their doctor's voice, on a ward round,
And seen my smile; they'll notice who it is
Under the outfit when I come again
As Father Christmas. Well, here goes . . .' No sound
Escapes my lips at the first bed; small fingers
Reach for the offered joy; each counterpane
Becomes a magic carpet. A fat boy
Gives me a wink: 'I've seen you!' His glance lingers.
'Today?' I ask – but that's not what he meant;
'No; last year, at Christmas.' Grabbing his toy,
He thanks and greets me as a long-lost saint.

*Edward Lowbury*

# Clinical clerihew (4)

SIR JAMES SIMPSON

Sir James Simpson and his staff
By inhaling a pint and a half
Of chloroform, almost had a seizure;
And quite by chance invented anaesthesia.

*Christopher Mann*

## Night Star

I woke up coughing in the night
And wondered just where I could be.
There was an overhead dull light
But it was still too dark to see.
I felt some little pangs of fright
Before it all came back to me.

Because then I did remember
That I lay in a hospital bed.
'When you were ill, we brought you here.
You're so much better now,' they said.
'Three more days for the germs to clear.
Home, and your favourite bedspread.'

I felt so small in this big bed.
How enormous the world must be.
Thoughts went round and round in my head.
Perhaps there's no-one else but me.
Or was I someone else instead?
Was this long night Eternity?

And then I saw a little light.
A friendly voice said, close to me,
'I heard you coughing in the night.'
And she talked to me quietly,
'I came to see that you're all right.
Why don't we share my cup of tea?'

I opened my eyes and it was day
And the sun shone glowing and bright.
My Nurse of the Night had gone away
Like the stars which fade in daylight.
And at my side my breakfast tray;
A fresh boiled egg, smooth and white!

I see green trees, not very far,
Blue sky and clouds all shining white
Floating above the window bar.
And when the dark hides them from sight,
My Night Nurse, like the Evening Star,
Will come to watch me through the night.

*Robert Sparrow*

## Superfluous surgery

*He*:   'One's tonsils are dispensable,
         Or so the surgeons say,
         So why not just be sensible
         And take yours out today?

         One's appendix is expendable,
         It's proved beyond a doubt;
         It would be most commendable
         Of you to take *yours* out.'

*She*:   'Your brain is quite ridiculous,
         As far as I can tell,
         So why not be meticulous,
         And take *that* out as well?'

                                        *Colin West*


# A surgeon from Glasgow

A surgeon from Glasgow named Mac,
Once forgot to put everything back.
As his train made to start,
His case came apart,
And a kidney rolled down off the rack.

                        *Michael Palin*

## 'This one is ill'

My throat
is a kaleidoscope
of red hot nails and broken glass.
I cannot laugh
or eat, or drink
or sleep, or think.

People come.
'Oh, look at this one!'
This one's much too old,
her hands are rough and cold
with purple gooseflesh ending in a paper frill;
she whispers hoarsely over me, 'This one IS ill.'

At night
I fight
the sharp rocks rolling round my feet
with soggy twisted sheets.
The whispers echo in my head,
typewriters chatter round my bed.

A morning comes when I am cool;
the wet is dry and rough is smooth.
She gives me chicken jelly on a spoon
and whispers kindly, 'You may be going home quite soon.'
The sheets are friendly too, without the creases.
I sit up, to see a jigsaw puzzle with a thousand pieces.

*Jane Whittle*

# We went to see our Gran today

We went to see our Gran today,
we went to see our Gran;
in the big white-clean hospital
where the nurses smile
and speak in soft voices.

We went to see our Gran today,
we went to see our Gran,
in the big sunshiney room
where the old people sit in chairs
and say nothing to the television.

We went to see our Gran today,
we went to see our Gran,
in the little room with the shiny metal things
and the big white curtains.
I showed her my drawing of our cat in the rain,
and it made her cry.

We went to see our Gran today,
we went to see our Gran;
but today she didn't say anythng,
she didn't even say hello,
she just smiled
and her eyes were bright.

We went to see our Gran today,
we went to see our Gran,
in the dark room next to the doctor's.
She was sleeping,
and her hands were cold,
and the nurses were very quiet
and quickly drew the curtains.

*Christopher Mann*

## Ella McStumping

Ella McStumping
was fond of jumping.
From tables and chairs,
bookshelves and stairs
she would jump to the floor
then climb back for more.
At the age of three
she climbed a high tree
and with one mighty cry
she leapt for the sky.
Doctor McSpetter
says she'll get better,
and the hospital say
she can come home next May,
and Ella McStumping
has given up jumping.

*Michael Dugan*

## In hospital

Doctors hurrying,
Nurses scurrying
And me worried in my room.

Doctors talking,
Nurses walking
And me listening in my room.

Doctors looking,
Nurses watching
And me lying in my room.

Doctors standing,
Nurses waving
And me going to my home.

*Edward Mooney (7)*

90

# Last Word

## Curing song

Your heart is good.
(The Spirit) Shining Darkness will be here.
You think only of sad unpleasant things,
You are to think of goodness.
Lie down and sleep here.
Shining darkness will join us.
You think of this goodness in your dream.
Goodness will be given to you,
I will speak for it, and it will come to pass.
It will happen here,
I will ask for your good,
It will happen as I sit by you,
It will be done as I sit here in this place.

*Yuma Indians, North America*

# Acknowledgements

The editor and publishers would like to thank the following for permission to use copyright material in this collection. The publishers have made every effort to contact the copyright holders but there are a few cases where it has not been possible to do so. We would be grateful to hear from anyone who can enable us to contact them so that the omission can be corrected at the first opportunity.

The Bodley Head Ltd for 'Sickness does come' by John Agard from *Say it all again, Granny* by John Agard.

Cadbury's National Exhibition of Children's Art – Poetry Section for 'Cough cough cough' by Oliver Gray; 'Mumps' by Nicola Jane Field; 'Thoughts from a dentist' by Amanda Evans; 'Having a brace' by Karen Elkington; 'My head' by Erika Cottle; 'A visit to the doctor' by Robin Gillyon; 'You can take my blood out' by Edward Cooper; 'A thought' by Mark Raven and 'In hospital' by Edward Mooney. All poems appear in the *Cadbury's Book of Children's Poetry* (vol 1–6), published by Beaver Books, Century Hutchinson Ltd.

Carcanet Press for 'A charm against tooth-ache' by John Heath-Stubbs.

Century Hutchinson Ltd for 'Superfluous surgery' by Colin West from *It's funny when you look at it* and 'A surgeon from Glasgow' by Michael Palin from *Limericks*.

William Collins for 'Invalid' by Gareth Owen from *Song of the city*.

John Collis for 'Job satisfaction'.

Jenny Craig for 'Asthma attack' © Jennifer Curry.

Jennifer and Graeme Curry for 'Visit to the dentist' from *Down our street*, published by Methuen Children's Books.

Andre Deutsch Ltd for 'Calling the doctor' by John Cunliffe from *Standing on a strawberry*.

Peter Dixon for 'Chicken spots' from *Big Billy*, published by Sarsen Press, Winchester.

Gerald Duckworth & Co Ltd for 'Henry King' by Hilaire Belloc.

Gavin Ewart for 'Sniffle skiffle'.

U A Fanthorpe for 'Children imagining a hospital'.

Four Winds Press for 'Wendy in winter' by Kaye Starbird from *The covered bridge house*, published 1979.

Tym Hatterley for 'French air'.

J. B. Lippincott for 'Measles' by Kaye Starbird from *Don't ever cross a crocodile*, published 1963.

Longman Cheshire Pty Ltd for 'Ella McStumping' by Michael Dugan from *My old Man* (Trend Series 76).

Edward Lowbury for 'Dr Christmas'.

Lutterworth Press for 'Be careful' by Richard Edwards from *The word party*.

Macmillan & Co for 'When Dad felt bad' by Charles Causley from *Little nippers*.

Wes Magee for 'Tracey's tree' and 'An accident'.

Christopher Mann for 'Spots'; Clinical clerihews 1, 2, 3 and 4; 'We went to see our Gran' and 'It's cold in our room'.

Methuen Children's Books for 'Sneezles' by A. A. Milne from *When we are six*.

Barry Norrington for 'Tom's song'.

Gareth Owen for 'A stomach-ache is worse' from *Salford Road*, published by Penguin Books.

Penguin Books Australia Ltd for 'Dad's pigeon' by Doug Macleod from *The fed-up family*.

G P Putnam's Sons for 'My nose' by Dorothy Aldis from *All together*, copyright 1925–28, 1934, 1939, 1952, renewed 1953, 1962, 1967 by Dorothy Aldis.

John Rice for 'When I telephoned' from *Zoomballoomballistic*, published by Aten Press.

Vernon Scannell for 'Nettles'.

Robert Sparrow for 'A-shoo!'; 'Feeling great!'; 'All aboard'; 'Big day'; 'Hardly himself' and 'Night star'.

Anthony Thwaite for 'The Kangeroo's Coff' from *Allsorts 3*, edited by Ann Thwaite.

Shaun Traynor for 'Spots!'; 'What's wrong with me?' and 'Ear-ache'.

Walker Books Ltd for 'Sniff' by Colin McNaughton from *There's an awful lot of weirdos in our neighbourhood*. Text and illustrations copyright 1987 Colin McNaughton. First published in the UK by Walker Books Ltd.

Jane Whittle for 'Limerick in bed'; 'And how are we today?' and 'This one is ill'.

Ian Whybrow for 'Well, ill' and 'Headache'.

# Index of first lines

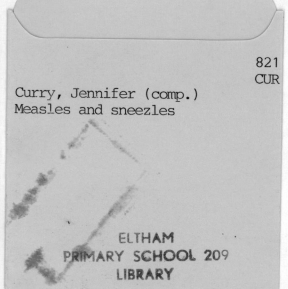